killer 7

Order this book online at www.trafford.com
or email orders@trafford.com

Most Trafford titles are also available at major online book retailers.

Printed in the United States of America.

ISBN: 978-1-4269-2644-0 (sc)
ISBN: 978-1-4669-2342-3 (e)

Trafford rev. 09/20/2011

www.trafford.com

North America & international
toll-free: 1 888 232 4444 (USA & Canada)
phone: 250 383 6864 ♦ fax: 812 355 4082

†

In Africa a team of archeologist scientist's where digging for fossils but instead of finding fossils they found something that was very unusal it was some sort of alien device they decided to take it back to New York City at the E.S.Q Labs for research and the more they research the more they became determine to learn the aliens device secrets a scientist name professor Adrian Greenwald accidentally activated the recording mechanism it showed him Images of the past in another galaxy where the beast warriors where slaughtering other alien race also he saw the beast planet devouring alien planet's after the invasion he saw that the beast planet only purpose in life was to travel the stars and devour the planets it comes a cross after witnessing all of the destruction he became skeptical about he's alien discovery but what he did not know is that beast warriors can sense their technology being used and the location of it's where about so he's life was know in danger he just doesn't know it yet !

Knight mare

The power of the beast is close I can feel it ha h a h a

It's 400.000 years ago since we have crash landed on this pathetic little mod ball and the power of the beast was lost to me but now the power has risen again for me to posses

Strife

Sir according to the ships scanners the orb of the beast is located on the north west New York city sir

Knight mare

Full speed ahead

Professor Adrian Greenwald

Starting to give off a strange reading but why the lab computers is going crazy

I bet it's because of this strange device

1

Knight mare

Wind guard strife all of you engage the E.S.Q labs

Suddenly the ceiling came falling down and in came the beast warriors they began there assault on the lab

Strife

Tear and rip this lab to pieces until you find the beast stone

Black vain

Strife I found some humans pest what should I do kill them

Strife

yes kill them immediately they are useless

Then from strife communicator Knight mare voice

Shouted

Knight mare

No strife you fool ask them about the stone of the beast

Black hart

And then we can kill them boss

Knight mare

yes but only after you retrieve the stone

Black hart

Oh yes ha ha ha

In the middle of the chaos Dr Greenwald and all the other scientist where trembling with fear

Wind Guard

Shut up and tell us where the beast stone is

Right after Wind Guard statement another explosion came from the main entrance

Narks had finally arrived at the seen

Strife

Who the hell are these guys !

Prime

Where Narks and your shit out of luck when you decided to attack this lab and the humans working here

Strife

You assholes think you can stop us you are all dead

Dark sector attack the fight began between the two teams

Each team started showing off there special powers but during the fight.

Wind guard

Going somewhere professor Greenwald your coming with me show
Me where you put the beast stone

Greenwald

What is a beast stone and how did you know my name

Wind guard

Not that it's any of your business but mind reading is one of the special powers

Given to me by the beast and I also know that I kneed your eyes for the retinal scanner

now you do it willingly or I can rip out your eye sockets

Greenwald

No No ! please don't hurt me I'll do it just give me one second

Wind guard

Ah there it is the precious beast stone at last four hundred thousand year old search is now over the power of the beast will be ours again. Now human that your use fullness is over it's time to die any last wards

Greenwald

Yes why is this beast stone as you described it so important?

Wind guard

Well human if learning about the beast is your final wish then so be it I will tell you

Eons ago before your worthless planet even had life far away in another galaxy there was a great war between two very powerful alien race they where called the nark's and the beast warriors. We the beast warriors and the narks entered your solar system the battle carried on until finally the two battleships are shot down each other. We crash landed on this stinking ball you call Earth and in the middle of the struggle we lost the hart of the beast.

And now after thousands of years here we are again with the hart of the beast

Greenwald

But you still have not told me anything about why the stone is so important to you

Then nightmare from wind guard communicator says

Knight mare

Wind guard have you located the beast stone yet

Wind guard

Yes you're Excellency

Knight mare

Then bring it to me at once let no one stand in your way because once I have it I will use

it to call down the beast and then the beast will become even stronger then ever right after it devours this planet

Greenwald

That's the reason why your after the alien device I wont let you destroy earth

Knight mare

Wind guard who the hell was that kill him right now

Right after that another explosion came from the corner a never before seen nark warrior had just made a entrance could he be the one to save professor Greenwald and prevent the beast warriors from taking away the hart of the beast that will also mean the near destruction of earth..

River

Hold it right there

Greenwald

Please whoever you are stop him he's going to destroy us all

Wind guard

It's time to die you snitch take this

As Wind guard was getting ready to take aim an interceptions came from Adonis

By using a bio energy beam from his hand to knock down wind guard

Back on the spaceship that is hovering over the E.S.Q labs after realizing that wind guard

Has bin taken out by one of the narks he ordered one of his men to fire on the lab full energy but only after he teleported the rest of he's men out of there he would rather destroy them then to let them get their hands on the stone right after his space ship toke off

Narks burst out of the ground

Maverick

Those beast fools are goanna pay for this right now

Prime

No

Maverick

Say what

Prime

This man is hurt badly if we don't get him some help right away he will die and I don't have the time he seems to know what the beast where after. I want know it too so let's move the cop's are on there way.

Back at the Nark seven building

Maverick

Prime this man that you have place in the infirmary who is he why don't we hand him over to a real hospital

He knows why Knight mare and the rest of the beast where at the lab

now I'm going to revive him with this neo recovery

Greenwald

Where am I who are you strange looking people you half to let me go to the police

Something serious is about go down this could be the end of mankind as we know it

Prime

Clearly you know why those men attack the lab would you mind letting me know you see we are Nark seven and we have dealt with those men before

back at ground zero. The F.B.I and clean up crew where on site but then one of the

Clean up crew agents discovered the alien stone then handed it over to one of the F.B.I

Agents so they decided to take it with them for more thorough investigation.

Agent Bishop

Well so far we know this thing is not from earth that much where sure of

What I want to know is how did it get here I think I need to make a phone call

Excuse me. Hello general remember when you where telling everyone about the time you

Thought you have seen a U.F.O Space Ship well I got the proof you need to back up your clams.

General Foxx

Pleas tell me more agent bishop

Later that day

Bishop

Glad you could make it General now since our highly advance peace of hard ware I

Decided to go a head and call in the world best techno Scientist I'm sure your familiar

With The famous maverick from nark seven with his expertise I know that we will have a better Understanding on this peace of alien stone.

Maverick

Thank you agent Bishop General I'm very excited to be here I'll do my best to make you all proud.

Foxx

Very good Maverick glad to hear listen to me Bishop unlike the rest of you idiot's

I never like or trusted nark 7 and know you brought one of them on board

Maverick

Is everything all right agents are you still going to show me the stone?

Bishop yes of course with out further ado here is the alien stone

Maverick

Prime was right about the humans having it they have no idea just how dangerous that really is.

Later that same day it was breaking news report was that killer seven had completely

Destroyed new York killing thousand of people there was footage of killer 7 destroying the city

Back at killer 7 headquarters the alarm went off right after a response from the communicator   to confirm to maverick about the mission it was a success.

Maverick

Yes prime but something wrong is happening the human are attacking me.

Prime

What!

Maverick

Yah I'm under heavy fire Sir I'll do my best to stay alive sir scorpions every Where ahhhhh

Prime

We lost he's signal but I don't need it I know exactly where he is after all I'm the one that

put him on this mission so if anything happens to him I'll never for give my self.

Alright team where heading to that government facility Maverick needs our help bad .

Adonis

Ah excuse me Prime I think you should definitely have a look at this where on T.V

And it's real bad according to that news report the whole world looks destroyed look at all of New York This is crazy Prime .

Goliath

Prime what are we going to do?

Prime

I'll tell you what where going to do where going down there and kill whoever is

responsible Maverick my old friend I'm sorry but you'll have to wait there are thousand

people suffering in New York or what's left of it. When this is over I'll avenge you

When killer seven showed up in the real killer 7 jet battles between the two jet battles in the sky was intense the imposters and there ship decided to retreat at full speed

Shinn

Sir they are retreating and according to my scanners there are at least five thousand people Dead three thousand are still alive but are in critical condition.

Prime

Ok Shinn thanks for your report now team let's get out there and help these people.

As killer seven began the rescuing all of the civilians   right at time square the breaking News was interrupted by no other then Knight mare himself.

Karnack

Oh my god look you guy's Knight Mare just took over the news report what the fuck is he Up to

Quail

I don't know Karnack but you can bet he's up to no good let's listen to what he has to Say

Knight mare

Hear me people of the world my name is Atlas and yes I am the alien from the stars we are here because we are intergalactic police men .We have been tracking a group of space

Criminals who calls them self killer 7

Black shot

What! Prime this is bullshit we have to do some thing he's lying

Knight mare

Here me people of earth these are aliens who do not care about you or your children they

will destroy every thing in sight and any human that survive will be turned in to slave's if you human's don't help us destroy killer 7 this will be the end of mankind as we know it.

If there are any state officials that is interested in saving his people he's coulter

They animals your planet everything but it does not have to be this way just contact me at

These coordinate

Karnack

Prime we have to do something Knight Mare is trying to scapegoat this is such a

Mess. I would have never thought things would of been this bad man just when things can't get any worst .

You guy's the military forces are coming for us.

Prime

They just open fire all of you take cover now

As earth military defense force began there assault prime realized this was all a

Set up by his long time arch enemy Knight Mare he then swore that he would make them

pay for what he's done if only he can get himself and the rest of his team out of the away from the attack.

Meanwhile

Back at the F.B .I secret research facility the hero Maverick is now considered an

Intergalactic terrorist now he is fighting for his life but still does not know why these

Special F.B.I swat team called the Black scorpions to attack him he fought back

taking down scores of them before he was finally captured by the black scorpions .

Foxx

How the mighty have fallen hey Maverick did you and the rest of killer 7 think you could get away.

by destroying all of New York city and the world tomorrow.

Let's get one thing clear I' never like you or the rest of your killers I always knew that

Someday soon you and the rest of your team will try and trick us by pretending to be

Hero's with a add bonus you provide us with your advance technology where would I Get a idea to think up such incredible device no one from earth can hey Maverick !

did you really think you could honestly fool me you may have been able to fool the world

but not me because I'm about as sharp as a razor blade. You are going to have to try harder .

Then that alien scum

Maverick

Alien you have completely lost it Foxx everybody knows there are no such things as

Aliens tell any one that crack and they would laugh at you for it. Now let me go and I'll

for get all about this ok

General Foxx

Ha ha ha ha so nobody is going to believe me ha well lets turn on the news see how the world thinks about you Narks now

As Maverick pay attention to the news report he started to understand that the secret

About him and his team and what's been revealed his team had always felt more like a family then just an intergalactic military team.

From the planet Nark 7 for thousands of years him and the rest have manage to keep the secret about who

they really are even five years ago when they first became famous world never

would have thought humans that aliens are living among them the humans use to thank them by give them keys to the city

build museums even made movies. based on them and now all of that came crashing down. The heroic team of seven are outcast and are public enemy number 1 the

entire world now fears and hate them for everything they have done by killing innocent people

the lives they have taken away by the killer team they are now listed as wanted .

Maverick

No! it can't be not after every thing we have done for the humans listen to me Foxx

You have to let me go this is far too serious but it may not be to late those reports you hear are not true. The news report is completely incorrect   just give me a chance to

Then Foxx quickly interrupts maverick before he has a chance to say anything ell's

Foxx

Ha ha ha ha what in the hell kind of fool to you take me fore now I've hard a lot of stupid

Thing's over the years put this on is a new record ha   I've bin wanting for this chance

And it won't slip by now maverick I'm afraid that we have run out of fucking time there

Are other important things to attend to but don't you worrier I'll be back I promises you

Ha ha ha .

Just a few minute later General Foxx made a phone call to non other then Knight mare Him self

General Foxx

Master you where right all along you will be please to know that your plan is working out

Perfectly well killer 7 are no longer the world greatest hero's but they are the worlds most wanted

Knight mare

Excellent I knew everything would turn out just as I plan I will now gain the humans trust

By destroying the seven.

As the General continues with his conversation a young swat member named Tyler

Greenwald at time was on his way to a mission briefing when he over heard a very

interesting conversation from the General. As he began to listen to him it became more

clear there was something about Foxx than meets the eye as Foxx approached the

door to the room he was in Tyler knew he had to run off before it was too late.

As the day went on what Tyler heard kept playing inside his head things like

Taking over the world calling the other person on the phone master and disguising the

Plane he had for his old heroes. Now the narks are considered murders but now after over

hearing the conversation his mind has change back to the way it was before the

attack that made history.

Tyler Greenwald

Well if that was not them on the six o clock news then who the hell was it I got to get some

answers I know just were to get it but as for Foxx he is mix up in this can't trust

him anymore .

Killer 7 is now at a different location right after they made it back to H Q they fell under attack once again but the attackers where different a lot more skilled in combat

clearly these guys where being attack by pros. The 7 where able to hold there own

Get there valuables and escape the black scorpions and they where even able to activate

Self destruction sequence as they depart from there now old home base

Karnack

Well prime I got to admit that Knight Mare really nailed us pretty bad hah we lost

our home, we have lost the respect from the people of earth now we are a group of outcast.

The humans are calling us killer seven we lost most of our technology Back at H Q

Although that would not be so bad if maverick was still with us he can do anything when

It comes to technology in witch these humans have never seen .

River

Hay yah that's right in all these chaos I completely forgot about Maverick, Prime

you're the field commander what are you going to do there's no telling what these people will do to him

Black shot

Prime for once can you listen River is right we can't just leave Maverick with the FBI did you see how

difficult it was for all of us to hold are own against the Black Scorpions and Maverick

had to face them on his own. You know he had no chance at all but we are all physically linked to each other's mind we know he is still alive but the question is for how long.

problem if they decided to keep him locked up for the next 50 years they will notice

That he is not aging at all they might try to dissect him in order to find out what is the

secret to his body staying young and strong we can't let them do anything like that

Prime

Everyone calm down now listen up now I have not forgotten about maverick believe me I

want to save him just as bad as the rest of you. We can't just go barging in after him

And then start fighting we might harm the humans by attacking them to save Maverick all we

would be doing is proving to Knight Mare he is right sorry I can't let that happen we have to stop

and think of away to get him out of the F.B.I Head quarters don't worry he is coming

Back with us I promise.

Hmm.... excuse me but I just could not help but over hearing your little decision about a

Rescue mission allow me to introduce myself to you all.

before he could say another word the seven began shooting after him

Shin

Guys we have been discovered by one of the scorpion's kill him

The fight went on for the next five minutes black shot had him against the wall

just when he was about to finish him off Tyler screamed out

Tyler

Maverick sent me he needs your help badly please you have got to believe this I am telling the

truth about him

Black shot

Sorry kid your goanna have to do better then that   die

Prime

Black shot stop now that's an order so maverick sent you seeing everyone now

Hates us and want to kill us. You understand why my friend here is under a lot of

Pressure we all are but I have an idea one that can put everyone at ease

One of my team members has the power to read other peoples mind. He will let the rest of

Us now for sure that you are genuine when comes to telling us the truth about Maverick.

Quail come over here read his mind let us know if he can be trusted or not

Quail

Sure thing prime okay human listen well I need you to relax your muscles

put your mind at ease let nothing enter your mind that's it.

As Tyler cleared his mind Quail placed his hand on Tyler's head and began searching

Threw his thought and the where abouts of his friend and partner he had learn the truth

About Tyler and the where about of Maverick and then everything became clear then

He decided to fill in the others.

Quail

Alright you guys listen up it would seem are friend here is telling us the truth

He was sent hear by maverick. It would seem that he's got a little time left so we better

start figuring out away to get him out of there .

Tyler

Well I'm just glad that everything worked out finally now we can focus on more important

Matters. I can't believe you guys attack me how do you think I knew exactly where to find you guys if it was not for him

Prime

Please forgive us but it's just that you are dress like one of tough' Special Force soliders that

Attacked us earlier today and where under a lot of stress not only do we have to get

Maverick back but as leader I have to figure out away to stop Knight Mare and make him pay

For turning our life in to a Knight Mare .

Tyler

Look I wish I could help with your knight Mare problems but I'm afraid that if we don't Go after him we might be too late

Prime

O k then Tyler lead the way .

Now the team is sure about Tyler time can not be wasted but as they make there way

to the location were Maverick is being held captive there was more to this situation then

Prime ever imagine. His worst enemy had already anticipated his next move thanks to a

small spy robot that was keeping an eye on them the hold time. Back at the Beast warriors

Head quarters.

Knight mare

Well this is perfect thanks to the spy robot I can prepare a little welcoming party for

our friends well Foxx it would seem that you have a little rat in your department .

This is Tyler he has teamed up with my enemy's see to it that he is eliminated.

General Foxx

I just can't believe that one of our men is actually a traitor well he is going to pay with his life.

Meanwhile on the other side of town Killer seven show up at F.BI Head Quarters

Tyler

O.K you guys there are two security guard's at the main entrance any ideas on how to deal with them.

Shinn

Just leave everything to me watch as I morph into agent Bishop

Tyler

wow these aliens are incredible can't believe he actually has the ability morph completely in to another person .

security guard 1

Man I need a promotion so bad you think I should talk to the commander about this?

Security guard 2

Nah you'll probably just scare him with your ugly face

Security guard 1

Hay shut the fuck up

Fake Agent Bishop

soldiers I'm relieving you of your duties I'm putting you two on a mission with delta force your

to report sector G 9 immediately .

security guard 1

Finally got it

security guard 2

yah well I still say your ugly

Prime

Nice work Shinn very convincing now since you know this place pretty well Tyler lead the way.

As prime insisted that Tyler lead the way he lead the team to the elevator that took them to the very last floor

2 minuets later they where opening up the holding cell for Maverick

Maverick

Hey you guys actually made it boy it's been awhile Tyler look's like you came throw

Tyler

Yah it's a good thing too I bet anything these guys where planning something nasty

As Tyler and the rest of the team celebrate all except for there leader Prime

Prime

You know you guys this was all two easy no guards stood in our way it's all most like it's some kind of

then even before prime could even finish he's sentence Knight mare and his own troops where throw the door right behind him

Knight mare

Trap ha ha well you are very right Prime you have always been very smart how annoying and now down to business I have come

to finish off every last one of you but I could not have done it without a little help from .

prime

Help from who?

Knight mare

Allow me to introduce you to my partner General Foxx

Prime

I can't believe this human would help a monster like this what do you have to say about this human.

Knight Mare

Nothing Prime just need him to help us retrieve the beast stone.

Prime

You have it now and this man help you achieve your Gold

General Foxx

It was a good deal you see the boss her promise to make immortal just like him and all I had to use was government resource to get my hands on the alien stone and then I will become immortal

Prime

you are a fool your dreaming if you think Knight M are is goanna make you immortal he is just using you how can you live if your planet is completely destroyed

General Foxx

what are you talking about

Prime

The beast stone is a signaling device that has the power to call down the beast planet when the beast is summon by Knight Mare your planet will be devoured

killing all life on earth it will happen . The beast planet has been surviving for millions of years

The lives of trillions life on other planet's and now thanks to you your planet earth will be next

General Foxx

Master it's not true is it please!

Knight mare

I'm afraid so Foxx and now that you know the truth I can't let you live too bad I was going to keep you around a bit longer but now that I have the stone. I have learned what is wrong with it I guess I don't need you anymore.

General Foxx

No you can't I'm suppose to be Immortal

Knight mare

Die

Knight mare raise his hand and fire bio energy beam that completely destroyed General Foxx right after that Prime and his team began fighting with Knight mare and his team It was long and intense battle the walls began to shake

there was great light   in every corner thanks to the energy beams that was coming from both sides .

Prime

before I send you to hell Knight Mare if have the stone then why haven't you used it yet

Knight Mare

Prime it would seem that some of the stones power has merged with the human that found it for us and he is here in the waiting cell

Black vain go after the professor he has some of the stone power inside of him do that while I take care of Prime .

Prime

say hello to fist Goliath Shinn stop black vain by any means there goanna try to summon the beast we can't let that happen .

As the battle went on Goliath and Shinn chase down black vain and his brother black hart but they where able to meet Greenwald

before they could be stopped

Black vain

Alright old man the time has come for you to be useful. To us this stone and hold it above your head then the stone will combine it's power with rest of the power that is inside of you

Greenwald

No ever since the stone has merged with my body and mind I have seen the history of the beast I know what will happen if I do this you can go ahead and kill me if you want to but I will never help you call the beast world .

Shinn

you heard the man noo dice

Goliath

Unlike the other's I don't play nice this is the only time I'm goanna tell you let him go

Black vain

Never

Just as he refuse a bullet came flying in splatter his brains

Black hart

Black vain no! Son of a bitch you did this you stinking human where did you come from all of a sudden

Tyler

The name is Tyler remember it and nobody pushes my dad around when I'm here

Goliath

No way is this man your father this very interesting

Black hart

I could not agree more got your old man now little fucking human you killed my only brother so I think I'll return the favor

Shinn

Stop him before ah

just when Shinn and they others where about to jump into action they where attack from behind with he's bio energy beam

Black hart

Master your here I thought you and the other's where taking care of Prime and his team

Knight mare

I was but I'm not wasting anymore time it's time to call the beast do you hear me old man take this stone and call down the beast right now

Greenwald

I will never help you monsters so go ahead and do your worst

Black hart

Master do you see that boy over there that's his son hold Greenwald hostage and I'll bet he will do as you ask.

Knight mare

Excellent idea Black hart look here old man you had better pick up that stone and begin or you can watch your son die

Greenwald

No leave my son alone I'll do as you ask Prime for give me Tyler I'm sorry

Greenwald pick up the stone holds it over his head the power from he's body combine with the remaining power from the stone

and a very enormous beam shoot straight up into the sky and then and then the sky begin to tremble dark clouds started to appear in the sky for awhile nothing happen and giant portal open in space the beast is just out side our planet and is just seconds away from begin to devour the planet

Prime

Knight Mare what have you done

Knight mare

Looks like your too late Prime it is the end of this world you have lost my formidable

Rival

Karnack

Prime Knight Mare is right this is the end for the human race and us along with planet Earth

Prime screams out no and then charged himself for his strongest attack and fired it right into Knight mare .

Wind guard

Everyone retreat and grab the master there is no need to stay here anymore our home awaits lets get back to the ship.

River

Karnack should we go after them ?

Karnack

No at least not yet we have bigger problems right now

Greenwald

No! oh my god what have I done by giving them what they wanted I just brought down the Apocalypse but I have to save my only son

Tyler Greenwald

Dad your o k thanks for saving me I thought I was a goner for sure but why did you not

tell me that you where mixed up with these aliens

Greenwald

Yes it all started during my trip to Africa but it would seem you have made some friends of your own now the world is about to end I wish I never found the blasted thing

Other wise none of this would be happening right now

Prime

That's enough we have to get moving not another second to lose we must kill Knight Mare

He's special commandos and the rest of his troops think it's all over but it ant over until It's over

Maverick

What do you mean Prime if your trying to tell us that it's not over until the fat lady sings .

Well I would say she just hummed a few bars

Prime

Just look at this

Prime held up strife's head showing beasts they looked frightened by judging the shocking look upon each of there Faces

Prime

Strife body was completely disintegrated by River which actually workout

because now that he provided me with excellent plan

Goliath

Wait just a minuet I could swear I saw strife leaving with the others

Prime

No that was Shinn I ask him to morph into Strife since the other members of Dark

Sector where busy fighting with the rest of you did not notice they had lost one of there team mates

Karnack

Hey don't for get black vain he's a goner too

Maverick

Oh I get it prime

Your using Shinn like mole right then after he's made it to there home base he will

report there location then he will show up and take them all out .

Black shot

Yes but even if we finish off Knight Mare and the rest were still dead because the beast planet is here

Prime

That's why we have to get Knight Mare quickly before he tells the beast planet to begin   it's feast

Tyler

Sorry you guys I feel like this is all my fault if it was for me being Knight mares hostage

none of this would be happening right now

Prime

Non sense this is our war my friend and I have been fighting against these guys long

before man even existed this war we have dragged you humans in to it

but time is wasting lets get back to the hide out

Agent Bishop

Hold it right there nobody is going anywhere not until I get some answers you freaks

Better start talking you all look human but I know better thanks to that one over There

Maverick

The names Maverick if things weren't so serious right now I'd make you pay for using me Like a Ginny pig

Bishop

Your all under arrest and I want to know what in gods name is that abomination up in the sky

Karnack

I'll explain everything and with my power I will show you the history of it all

Right after Karnack was able to prove to him that everything was true Bishop decided to

Let them go for now but if they manage to get through this they will have to Become enemy's again

Black shot

So now that Bishop and he's scorpion are following us what is the next step and hey

Prime do you think we can actually trust Bishop and his scorpions

Quail

No I'm afraid not you see because the apocalypse is here he will help but if we could just

Stop the beast he will try to capture us in order to

Just before Quail could even finish a signal came up on the ship computer screen

Black shot

All right looks like Shinn came through for us he is sending something

Primes

Hmm looks like coordinates for Knight mares Hide out this is perfect all right men this is

It our final mission this is the big one lock and load Knight Mare and the beast world are both going down the entire team began cheering

Black shot

I'm ready to kick some ass Prime

Prime

Good

Meanwhile back at Knight Mare's hide out

Knight mare

YES! Success feels so good Wind Guard get on the calm link and tell all personnel's to

Report to the Red Falcon we have stayed and fought against Prime's and his men's long enough.

It's time too go home and leave this world in ashes

Wind guard

Your wish is my command your excellence

As wind Guard makes the announcement every beast solder made there way to the Red

Falcon then began there launch in to space toward the beast planet

Fake strife

Master you will be please to know that we have just landed but there is one problem

knight mare

what problem? there is nothing that can stop me now it's too late where no longer on Earth

far away from Killer7

Fake Strife

Yes that is true you are no longer on earth but if you think you have gotten away from me

your sadly mistaken die monster you Killed my Father 15teen years ago

knight mare

Strife what the hell has gotten into you ah I will make you pay for this you traitor take this

Hold still so I can blast you ah

who shot me from behind

Cyclops

It was that guard over there your excellence I'll teach him some manners

knight mare

I'm surrounded by traitors

Fake Strife

Watch me change you fool now do you under stand

knight mare

You're Shinn

shinn

I'm afraid one of my pal killed the real Strife back in are last fight and you did not even know that now it's costing   you big time now strife is dead it has provided me with the perfect

cover to sneak in to your hide out and onto your mother ship the Red falcon and give you're actual location

away to my friends now they will join me on the trip back to the beast world you are so screwed

Knight mare

I hate you die you bastard

Prime

No night mare your fight is with me

Knight mare

You and your friends are all here you pretended be some of my troops dame you

All troops and the reminders of my dark sector will kill them all .

Prime and his killer 7 team attacked Knight Mare and once again a

Big struggle for victory and fight for the future but Knight Mare was still a very crafty

Opponent he was able to pull a power switch actually electrified the ground and shocked

everyone knocking them out cold .

Knight mare

Now that these fools are out of my way I can do what needs to be done

Knight Mare activated the machinery that tells the Beast planet to begin its feast on

The earth now that the devouring has begun the world has already fallen into chaos

But as for the human race there was nowhere to run and nowhere to hide this is the end Of man kind as you Know it

Prime

What have you done!

Knight mare

Ah Prime how good of you to regain consciousness I'm glad you could witness this

moment ha ha

Prime

I would not celebrate just yet you think your so smart huh you think you got everything in a bag

don't you well surprise friend when told Shinn to Impersonate Strife I also gave him

a little Invention it's one of Mavericks toys we have been waiting century's for this

opportunity and now this time the gadget will reprogram this maniacal abomination

away from Earth. Oh and just to make sure you or any on else threaten the earth or any

other planet again with this machine Mavericks made it so it would send the beast into depth

of space where it's left alone in limbo never to see the light again this is the end of the beast and

your team get back to the red Falcon get off this planet while you can Tyler.

Tyler

What about you prime you will be lost with the planet as well

Prime

Don't worry about me I'll escape in one of the Minnie jets after I kill Knight Mare

Got to make sure he stays behind so he will not tamper with the computer and so that

Human life will never be threaten again now leave that's and order

And with that last command the entire team took off eminently flew back down to earth What's left of it

Prime

Look Knight mare you see the cable letting go of earth it's all over it's just you and me

and anyone else that wants to join in the fight

Knight mare

You dirty son of a bitch you just totally screwed me out of my victory your dead prime

Battle between the two was more vicious then any other time for it now do or die

Wind Guard

My lord please attend to that infernal device I'll kill Prime

During the fight prime punch a hole in Wind Guard's chest and left him bleeding to

Death and then sealed off the room so there are no more interruptions

Prime

your wasting your time Knight mare once it starts there is no turning back

Knight mare

Well it seems that you are right you may have stop the beast but the planet earth is still in

Grave danger the beast conflicted way too much damage on that pathetic little mud ball

The earth will know blow up 5 minutes you see I understand the beast more than you

We may no longer have the chance to devour it but it looks like it will be destroyed

ha ha ha

beast computer

initiating warp speed

sound like the beast just took use into the abyss in to nothingness now pay attention to the

monitors look

prime could do nothing but watch the earth blow it was the biggest explosion he head

ever seen and there was nothing he could do

Knight mare

Ha ha ha we might have lost the war to you prime but you have lost so munch more you

Have lost the Earth you have lost the humans hate and fear you thanks to my

Scapegoat Game that I played but best of all of you had to witness death of each

And everyone of your Friends ha ha

Prime

Karnack Shinn Maverick Goliath Black shot River Tyler Professor Greenwald there all

Gone and it's all because of you

Your dead do you hear me ah

Then after that he began too transform releasing he knew he would need

All of his power to fight against Knight Mare prime was now on the attack fighting

Against Knight Mare the fight dragged on and on till they reached out side in to a city on

the beast planet

Knight mare

Darn how did you get so mighty all of sudden just because you change your Appearance

Prime

I always had this power but I rarely use it for a very good reason this may be

More then enough but at the same time my powers are eating away at my life if I don't beat you and change back in ten minutes then I'm dead so take this

Prime gave Knight Mare that rip through his stomach and out his back

Knight mare

NO! You think it's over but I still have one trick left see if you can block this attack

ahh

Knight Mare fired off a super charge energy beam at Prime then Prime send one of he's

Own and it soon became a test of strength between the two fighters but Prime strength

was too over whelming and it completely over power Knight Mare and rip his body into pieces

Knight mare was finally finish   for good

Prime

Yes I did it my friends I have avenge you all you can all rest in peace time to change back

Prime

Ah Blood I'm coughing out blood oh no it's been more then ten minutes it looks like this

is the end for me as well

and then just like everyone Prime could not hold on any more and he died as well

but all still was not lost at that very moment a mystical being appeared in front of Prime .

It' was and elder nark who is also the oldest nark there is he spent he's whole life

Traveling the stars and gaining wisdom   from trillion of different lives from other

planets and getting so much power that he now possess god like powers he witness

everything that took place

Elder nark

I have restored your life force brave warrior

Prime

What I'm alive but that is impossible

Elder nark

There very little things that are impossible for me

Prime

why did you revive me

Elder nark

Because such incredible good deed deserves to be rewarded I will restore all of your

friends just as I will restore you as well as the humans and the planet Earth. they did not deserve to be destroyed they where innocent by standards caught up in the

middle of your war with Knight Mare

Prime

Yes resurrecting me is one thing but this is an entire world where talking about can you

really do that

Elder nark

Be hold

Prime hey where not on the beast planet any more where back on Earth. We are back with all the people

all the people and every thing

Elder nark

Now you must keep your end of the bargain come with me for the next 50 years and master

Infinite wisdom as I have

Prime

Well it's a good thing that I am nark just like you elder other wise 50 years would of

been a problem good bye My friends I promise we will see each other again some day

The End of Chapter 1

It has been two years since killer 7 saved the human race from the beast planet now life

went back to normal. As for the team there life carried on being the best they

Could be they felt this is what their dead leader Prime would of wanted

Goliath

I can't help it Tyler I keep thinking Prime is going to burst through that door and start giving

Orders on what to do on our next mission or something like that

Tyler

Yeah I miss him to big guy but all we can do now is keep on fighting against criminals

Goliath

Tyler are you sure you want to be a part of killer 7 our life style is extremely dangerous

I think for your own safety you should just go back to being a black scorpion there you

will be fighting against normal criminals not monsters and mutants like us .Also

you are not immortal like we are you can die on these missions we will go on

Tyler

Your also forgetting that you and the rest may be immortal you forget that you are not

invincible so you can die too

Maverick

Excuse me gentlemen Karnack wants too see use all right now it appears to be some

Thing of great urgency

As the entire team gather around the mission in the briefing room

Karnack

My friends earlier today I learned about a team of mutants attacking Los Angeles

Black shot

Man! Another mutant attack that's the third time this month why

Karnack

But that's not all black shot these mutant don't seem too have any specific objective there

Just randomly attacking innocent people compounds homes place of business and no one

Knows why ?

Shinn

Well I for one would like to know when we are going to stop all this chit chat and get out

There and save the people and kick some mutant butt. While where at it

The team left there head quarters right after there meeting the team began feeling that

may be it was time for a new leader they could not bring them self to actually having

a replacement for prime. It was a very painful so they remain without a leader for

the next two years and kept on going without a leader

Quail

Ok team looks like we are in down town Los Angeles look they're down there

Goliath

Ok team let's get down there and show those ugly beast we mean business Tyler you

Better sit this one out this one goanna be tough

Tyler

No way had I come too far just to turn back now

Maverick

He's right kid this is not a joke stay here ok boy let's do this

Tyler

Yah sure let the weak human stay here

right staying here in this ship

Watching those Narks have all the fun to them selves

Tyler could do nothing but watch from the ship battle between the mutant and seven in a

Insane battle but the mutants prove to be more than a match for the team the mutants seem to know all of there moves and power

Tyler

Oh no guy's hang on I'm coming

Mutant solider 1

Well looks like you and your friends have finally reached the end of the road Quail because even though your immortal your still not invincible.

When the mutant solider was about to finish off Quail he was shot in the face by Tyler

Mutant 2

So it seem Killer 7 had there human friend stashed some where let's kill him now

As battle went on Tyler used his old fighting style against the mutants and some nark technology to help him win the fight over the mutant's

Adonis

I can't believe this Tyler you stop these mutate monsters by your self and us with all of

Our power could do nothing to harm these guy's.

Back at H Q the team was now finally ready to name there new field commander

Goliath

Well Tyler I'll be the first to say you prove me wrong you saved us all and to think I

Always thought that this job might be to dangerous for a human such as yourself

The mutants knew all of my fighting moves and powers.

Adonis

That's not all not only did they have all of are moves and fighting skills but they can

Use them better then we can.

Maverick

We will figure it all out later but right now I want to make an official announcement to

Tyler we think that you have just proven to us that you are just good of a nark solider

as we are. You have shown this entire team what takes to be a leader and team

player you have shown us what it takes for a human to be a nark solider so will you take up the

responsibility of being our new field commander

Tyler

I do and I won't let you guys down

Shinn

Well commander what will be our first move

Tyler

first let's see Maverick what do we know about these mutants any ways

Maverick

Well Sir we have learned another team of mutants are on the attack in the city of

Chicago some one has to stop this

Tyler

Something is not right here where are the black scorpions they handle crisis like this but there nowhere to be found

Maverick

Funny you should mention special forces Black scorpion we have a call coming in from

them right now

Tyler

Ok bring up the monitor lets see who trying to communicate with us

Terry

Tyler come in

Tyler Terry !Terry

Tyler listen I know your not one of us any more but we need help from you and killer seven

Where under attack there are mutant monsters everywhere don't know why there attacking us

Please Tyler you have too

Before Terry could finish saying what he need to the transmitter was cut off

Tyler

What's with these random attacks every minute there's another and another it doesn't make any sense at all but we'll figure it out later we have to go help before it's too late

The team left immediately but meanwhile at the secret H.Q of the black scorpion

Mysterious character

Thank you for your participation mister white I know the Seven will show up and fall right

In to my trap ha ha oh and let's not for get Terry your old partner is about to lose his life And all thanks to your betrayal

Terry

You wont get away with this you bastard

Mysterious character

As if anyone can stop me but anyways human I am getting sick of you so let me put a end To your life any last words

Terry

Yeah your about to get your ass kick look who's here

shinn

Alright freak this ends now

Tyler

Hey Terry are you ok

Mysterious character

Well how nice too see you all again you know I can hardly believe it 's

Been a while Tyler

Tyler

Who's there come out show and yourself

right there and then the mysterious man steps out of the shadow's Tyler and rest where all shocked when they saw it actually was

Tyler

General Fox this is impossible we all saw you die at the hands of Nightmare

Adonis

He blow you away with one of he's beam and now your back.

So all these random mutant attacks they where obviously you're doing you

Where trying to lower us out so that we can fall into your trap that's the truth isn't it

Fox

Well done inspector Adonis it seem you where able to see right through my little plan and

Since I have you all know I intend on killing you all as part of my plan and I think I

will start with this weak human

cybernetic fox broke terry's neck Tyler screamed out terry's name as he and the rest

charged after Fox the battle began the battle was ruff brutal and at time where even some

close calls

Shinn

Well black shot looks like where not going to make it out of this one alive huh ?

cybernetic solider has all kinds of weapon but some of them where beast technology

Black shot

Tyler we have too retreat this abomination is too much for us right know

Common kid there no sense in dieing on your first day as commander

Karnack

Look over there the mother ship is coming what is going on around here

Tyler

It's the destroyer but that but that enormous ship is only use for critical situation the

Scorpions must be taking this thing seriously look guy's it's about too fire on us get down

The ship began it's attack on the building fox decided it would be best if he retreat now

and get he's revenge later after that the ship landed and out came a another familiar face

It was agent Bishop leader of the black scorpions

Maverick

Bishop why are you helping us last time we cross path you where trying to kill us and

How the hell did fox rise from the dead I got a lot of questions and I know you got the

answers you brought him back from the dead did you

Bishop

Yes you are right we did bring him back from the dead. You see I always wanted to create our own super solider some one that could defend the human race from monsters like Knight Mare and his army of beast the old man knew that he's life was coming to end

he had cancer it made him bitter, angry and desperate for an answer for his predicament he

learned about our plans to create a cybernetic solider that could defend the world against

anything that would threaten humans. He decided to give us full permission to do as we

please with is body if he died from the cancer. So he got him self killed we did

what we thought was best for all mankind the one thing you can be sure of is that

fox's fear of dieing drove him insane he would do anything to live for ever he was

even willing to be Knight Mare's little bitch in exchange for eternal life but he was

betrayed and killed after that we where able to retrieve his body and thanks to the alien

technology we where able to bring him back bigger and better . General always

wanted to be immortal now he's getting his wish

Black shot attacks agent bishop and the wall

Black shot

You're the one that sent him after us trying to protect humans from us when are you going

to understand that we are the good guys this planet would be gone if it weren't for us you

and all the other humans would be in the belly of the beast if it weren't for us

Bishop

let go of me before I tell my men's to attack listen Fox this is a problem for us all know he

thinks he can save this world by causing a disaster on record high scale he is planning to

to use a nuclear missile fire them towards Washington D.C our guess he will be aiming at the

White House so when he finally nuke's Washington D.C the magnitude of that disaster will

Definitely cause the entire world will unite work together as one now and forever

Maverick

Bishop his actions are your responsibility you created that metal monstrosity and now

he's willing start world war 3. We have already fought in your world war 1 and 2 long

before you where even born and now this machine mutant is threatening the world again

Tyler

Alright team listen up where moving right now this is a red alert situation we have got to

infiltrate that machine mutant base of operations ok then lets move .

The team now had the biggest challenge they ever had to deal with since defeating the

living planet 2 years ago many of the team wish after this mission is complete may be it was time to go home to there own planet. Their was no point in

staying on earth anymore because they have finally destroyed the beast planet it's

been terrorizing them for million's of years but now that all life is safe the beast monstrosity.

We must get back to our planet besides people here hate and fear us leaving after this mission will probably be the best choice.

Quail

Hey check this out it's Foxx base of operation I wonder way in space though why so

high above the earth ahhh shit look fighter jets are coming out

It seem that Foxx had ordered his own team of air fighter to go out and stop the

Approaching enemies. The seven where now in a dog fight that seems to be a close call

for the team but Quail's quick thinking and Black shots straight shooting they where able

To beat the machine the mutants was able to throw at them .

Tyler

Ok quail full speed ahead we have to stop this mad man before it's too late

Ok now that we have landed let's go and find this guy and take him down

A shot came from the left and it almost hit Tyler in the head if it weren't for black shot

Diving down on him in order to save he's life

Black shot

Woo looks like we have company sevens defend your self's

The fight between the seven and the mutant solider went on for awhile but in the end they

where defeated and captured and taken away Foxx

Foxx

Welcome my friends you know I'm actually glad you are all here in the beginning

I thought it would be a big problem for me so I decide to try and eliminate you all but

first I needed to draw you out that why I kept sending my own troops out on random

Mission attacks. Once that happen I new you would all try

something heroic feared that killer seven after all you a stop the mighty knight Mare and

he's force but that was just the beginning isn't it even as far as to stop an entire world the

beast planet they only living planet known to us now that is quite a resume so you can

see how it felt that it was best for me to deal with you now before anything else

mutant solider

General the nuclear missile are armed and ready for deployment

Foxx

Excellent finally everything is going my way I have got what I always wanted to be

Immortal not the way I always planed but the important thing it is mine

Now so what if I'm more machine then man and now I'm about to bring peace to the

world by blowing it up. When I destroy Washington D C people will morn their love ones

that kind of disaster will unite people of the world then their will be no more fighting

among them selves

Adonis

You are one fucked up mother fucker the last time you where willing to destroy your own

Planet in exchange for immortality and now your talking about bring peace to humanity

50

Foxx

Their was more to me then meets the eye you see my original plan was to wait for

Nightmare to grant me eternal life then when that's over and done with I was going to

Betray him and stop him from signaling the beast

Adonis

But we'll never know that for sure will we in any case your willing to fire off nuclear

missiles because you think people will throw down their weapon and start loving each other

Foxx

Yes my alien friend I will be the savior of my planet and you all will die here and at my hands just to insure that everything goes according to plan.

Adonis

Your just a megalomaniac and I will stop you ah

The fight between cybernetic Foxx and the seven began once again they head to fight for

A world that was not their own a race of people that fared and hated them is right yet

They keep fighting to defend it why these are the thought that flow through the minds of the members

Foxx

Why do you keep fighting for a world that's not even you're the people of earth hate and

Fear you and that super swat team black scorpions want your head on a platter so why

Throw away your lives just leave now and go back to your own world or you can stay here and die

At that moment a powerful noise it was the nuclear missile have been launched

Tyler

Oh my god he fired off the missiles their aiming straight for Washington D.C all those

People their all gone and we could not even stop him

Foxx

You see your nothing without prime if Prime was still alive he would of done something

annoyingly heroic good thing he's dead ha .

The entire team attack Foxx with extreme prejudice the new Foxx has to die right

now they where all beaten down . He had the advantage his data showed him

all their moves and all of their powers he had them beat in every way. Death for the seven

it was only moments away then all of a sudden Foxx was blown away by high intense bio energy beam everyone screamed out prime

Maverick

Prime your alive but that "s impossible you died years ago the living planet blow up with you in it

Foxx

Prime so your back from the dead too I don't know how you appeared out of no where and I

don't care I'll finish you off with the rest I have data on you too your no match for me dieeee

fighting was intense but no matter how hard Foxx tried he could not lay one finger on

Prime the cybernetic super solider was completely out matched for

Foxx

Damn you I can't beat him you have always been like this Prime Nightmare said you where

No matter how big the challenge is you always step up to the plate but you must tell

Me where you came from all of a sudden

Prime

Dematerializing in order to travel through space and time was one of the first tricks I

Learned from the elder

Prime

You see Foxx your data does not work on me because I have evolved in to something

Much more powerful you have data on what I use to be

Foxx

It does not matter how much you learned and it does matter that I can't beat you I

already won. Washington is completely destroyed and the world will come to gather and

live in peace I will show them that fighting and having war will lead to their own

destruction

Prime

Yes but at cost of millions your not a savior you're a monster just like your old

Master Nightmare peace will come to the humans in time not through extreme force

I'm goanna make you pay for the millions of lives you took away

Foxx

you can't kill me

Now that I'm a machine mutant I am immortal just like you but unlike you I am

Invincible

Prime

Invincible are you sure because I can still hear a hart beat

Words is after that statement prime punched foxx into his chest his fist pierced he's robotic armor

Then he grabbed his hart held in his face crushed it putting a end to Foxx's life

His body fell to ground and it was finally over

Karnack

Prime you stop him it's finally over but these new powers of yours where did you learn them

The entire team gather around him wondering where has he been after all this time

little did they know this was no time to catch up because Foxx was still not

Finish.

Foxx

Back up power baby it's not over until I say it's over so take this

Foxx fired of beam that pierced a hole in Tyler chest the rest of the team screamed out

He's name Tyler's life was now in critical condition

Foxx

And now to deal with the rest of you I just activated the self destructive sequence I'm

Taking you all to hell with me

Shinn

Everyone out now we have a few a seconds holy shit well never make it in time

Goliath

You know I'm getting tired of this guy blowing things up around me

The space tower exploded and destroyed everything but meanwhile

Back on earth

Black shot

What where back on earth but how prime? How did you bring us back

Prime

Yes just in the nick of time that crazy Foxx almost killed us all lucky for us he

Failed

Maverick

But he did get one of us Tyler is dead poor kid you know prime he took your position when

We all thought you where dead but now he's gone

Prime

No I can still sense he's life force and that is good enough for me to revive him

Tyler chest was healed the hole in his chest was gone now he   got up and said

Tyler this is   impossible I'm pretty sure Foxx blew me away

Back shot

Yes but prime saved you as matter fact he saved us all from that crazy bastard

Tyler

Well now that we are all fine we should start worrying about what to do

with the lost of Washington it's gone what happens now

shinn

Prime do you think you can take us back to our base

Prime brought them all back to their home base they made contacts with other world

Leaders by coming up with a plan

The human race became sick of the violence weapons where thrown down by other country's

Dismantle all their nuclear missile there was virtually no weapons and no more fighting

Different race of people came together humanity realize they where almost

completely wiped out first by the a living planet then secondly by a super solider

that was made   to defend the earth but instead decide to destroy mankind

The End